Two Is for Twins

Wendy Cheyette Lewison
pictures by Hiroe Nakata

VIKING

VIKING
Published by Penguin Group
Penguin Young Readers Group, 345 Hudson Street, New York, New York 10014, U.S.A.
Penguin Group (Canada), 90 Eglinton Avenue East, Suite 700, Toronto, Ontario, Canada M4P 2Y3
(a division of Pearson Penguin Canada Inc.)
Penguin Books Ltd, 80 Strand, London WC2R 0RL, England
Penguin Ireland, 25 St Stephen's Green, Dublin 2, Ireland (a division of Penguin Books Ltd)
Penguin Group (Australia), 250 Camberwell Road, Camberwell, Victoria 3124, Australia
(a division of Pearson Australia Group Pty Ltd)
Penguin Books India Pvt Ltd, 11 Community Centre, Panchsheel Park, New Delhi – 110 017, India
Penguin Group (NZ), Cnr Airborne and Rosedale Roads, Albany, Auckland 1310, New Zealand
(a division of Pearson New Zealand Ltd)
Penguin Books (South Africa) (Pty) Ltd, 24 Sturdee Avenue, Rosebank, Johannesburg 2196, South Africa

First published in 2006 by Viking, a division of Penguin Young Readers Group

3 5 7 9 10 8 6 4 2

Text copyright © Wendy Cheyette Lewison, 2006
Illustrations copyright © Hiroe Nakata, 2006
Library of Congress cataloging-in-publication data is available
ISBN: 0-670-06128-X

Manufactured in China
Set in Grumble
Designed by Kelley McIntyre

For Beth and Rob,
two of my favorite people
—W.C.L.

To Koharu
—H.N.

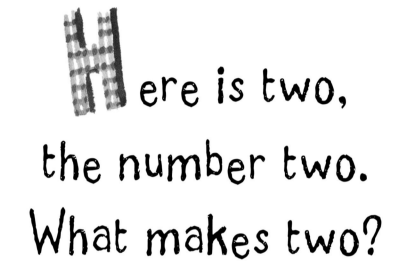

Here is two,
the number two.
What makes two?

Two hands do!

Two hands make two to hold a cup.

Two
eyes
look
down.

Two
eyes
look
up.

Two ears can hear a jingly sound.

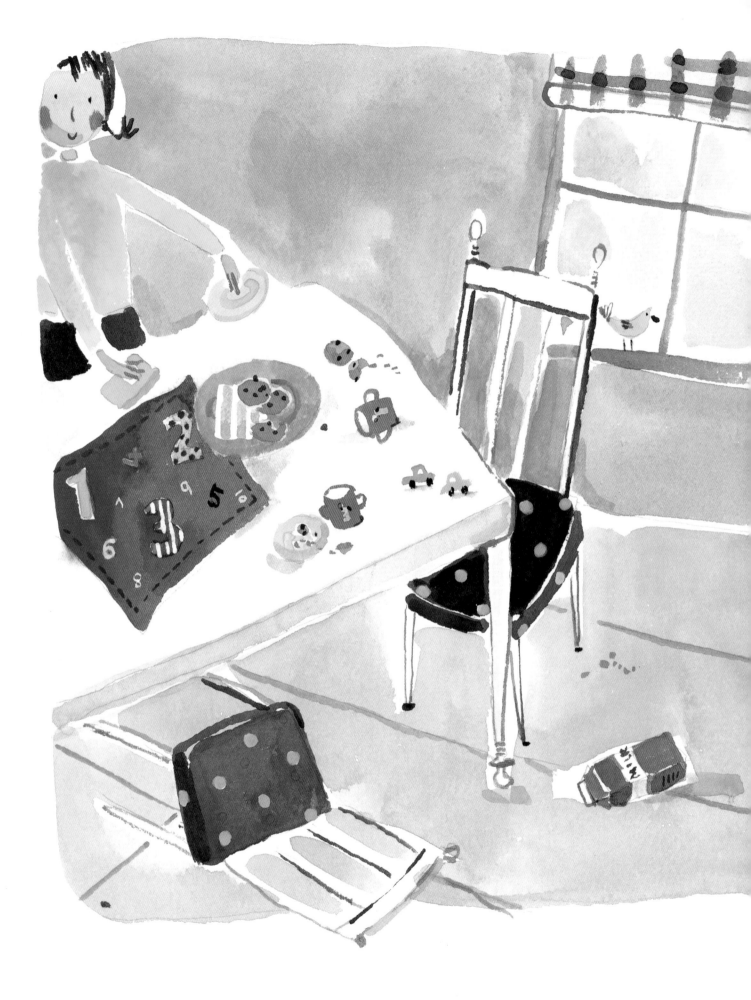

Two little feet dance all around.

What makes two?
All sorts of things!
A bicycle's wheels.
A bluebird's wings.

And twins, as you can plainly see,
are just as two as two can be.

TWO!

Sometimes they wear matching clothes.

Then they're two from nose to toes.

Sometimes they prefer to do
different things—and that's fun, too.

Still, twins are two without a doubt.
Twins are two inside and out!

Each one has the other there

to play a game . . .

to help . . .

to share.

Two
ride the
seesaw.

Two
build with
blocks.

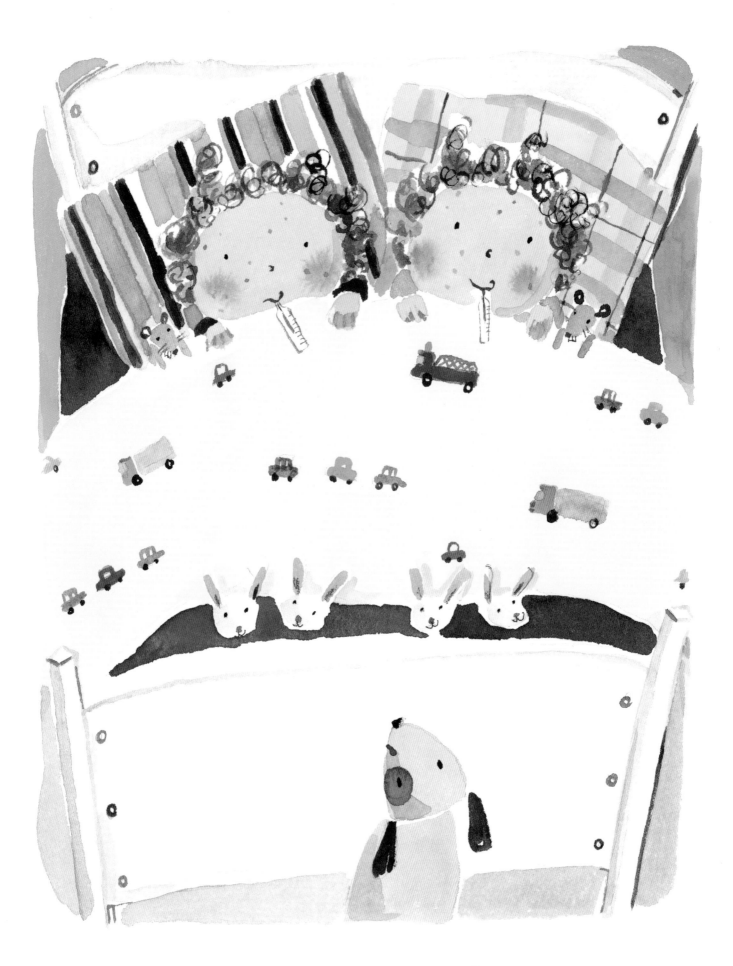

Sometimes two get chicken pox!

Twins are two-er than anyone.

Two times the hugs, two times the fun.

So on their birthday, Mommy makes . . .

can you guess?

Two birthday cakes!

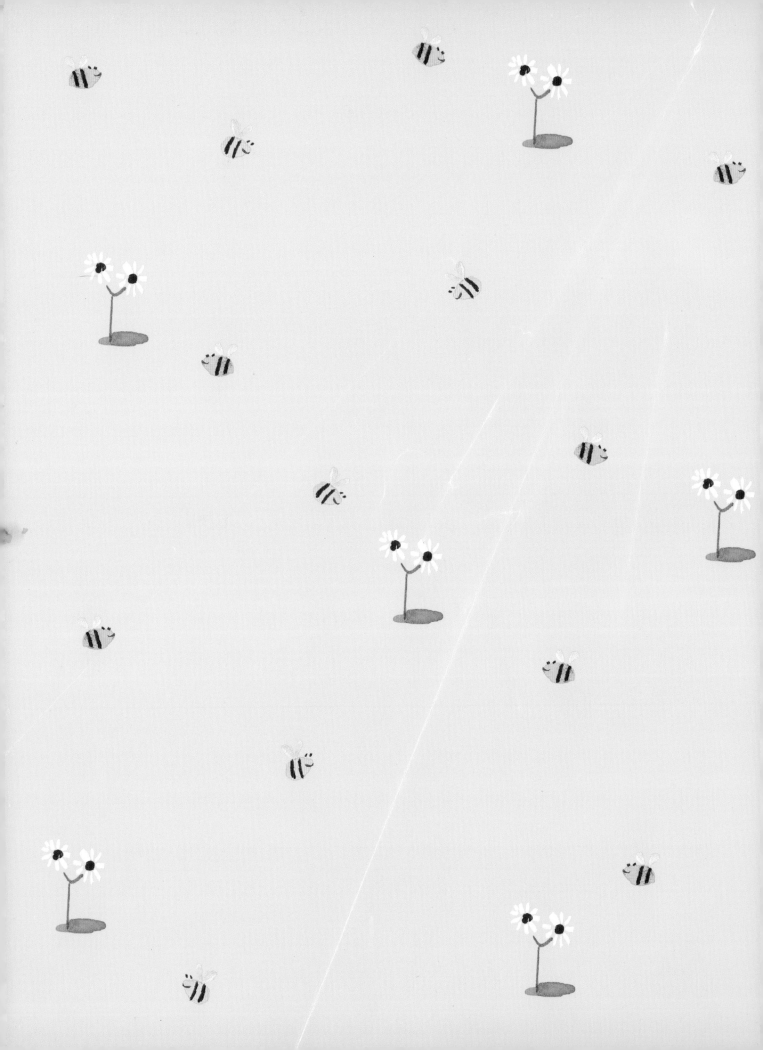